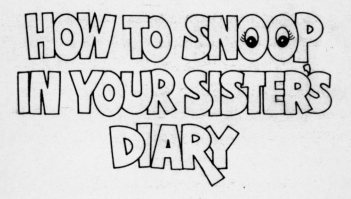

HOW TO SNOOP IN YOUR SISTER'S DIARY

by Janet Adele Bloss

illustrated by Don Robison

Published by Willowisp Press, Inc.
401 E. Wilson Bridge Road, Worthington, Ohio 43085

Printed in the United States of America
10 9 8 7 6 5 4 3 2 1

ISBN 0-87406-390-6

To Terry and Jill

One

"SCHOOL'S out! School's out!"
"It's summer vacation!"
"Yeah!"

Kids were busy cleaning out lockers, yelling good-bye to each other, and jumping for joy because the school year was over. Haley Sue Boster tucked a stack of books under her arm and crossed the hall to where Anna, her best friend, was cleaning out her locker. Anna was busily gathering up her collection of half-used pencils.

"Hi, Anna," she said. "Are you ready?"

"Sure," Anna replied as she stuffed her pencils into her backpack. "Let's go."

Haley and Anna hurried down the hall.

They stepped outside into sunshine, and heard shrieking from their classmates.

"You'd think we were being let out of prison," said Haley. "Everyone's going nuts!"

Suddenly, a hand plopped down on top of Haley's head and tugged on one of her curls.

"Ouch!" she yelled, turning around to see who the hand belonged to. "Scott Bailey, you keep your hands off of me!"

"Hey, Mop Top," teased Scott. "Where'd you get those curls? Did you stick your finger in a light socket?" He snickered at his own joke despite Haley's nasty looks.

Haley sighed and shook her head. Large, black curls bounced against her cheeks.

"Get lost, creep!" growled Haley. She clenched a fist and held it under Scott's nose.

"Ha!" exclaimed Scott. "Don't make me laugh." He held up his arms as if protecting himself from an attacker. "Oooooooo," he said. "You're really scaring me!"

Haley rolled her eyes, and looked over at

Anna. "He's such a hopeless case. Maybe we'd better call his doctor," Haley suggested.

Haley lifted her chin into the air, and started to walk faster. She and Anna took off down the sidewalk, leaving Scott behind.

"I can't believe what nerds boys are," said Haley.

"You can say that again," Anna agreed. They gave each other a knowing look and smiled.

Kids were scattered all around the school, talking in groups and tossing notebooks into the air. Cars and buses pulled out from the school parking lot.

"Just think!" Haley exclaimed. "We'll be in sixth grade next year. Can you believe it? I can't wait."

"You're both still babies compared to *me* ," said a boy's voice.

Haley whirled around to find Scott Bailey still tagging along closely behind her. "Who are you calling a baby?" she demanded angrily.

Scott pointed a finger from Haley to Anna and back. "You're both babies to me," he said, "because *I'm* going into *seventh grade* next year."

Scott puffed his chest out to make himself look bigger and more important. "If you think we're such babies, then why are you following us?" asked Haley. Her eyebrows shot upward as she waited for an answer.

Scott looked from Haley to Anna. Then he looked down at his feet. Tracing a line on the sidewalk with the toe of his shoe, he couldn't think up a quick answer. "Well, uh, maybe because there's nothing else to do," he said finally.

"Come on, Anna," Haley said as she shot Scott one last irritated look. Then she and Anna continued their way down the sidewalk.

"Is he following us?" asked Anna.

"Don't look back," whispered Haley. "Or else he'll know we're talking about him."

The girls walked in silence for a while.

Then, carefully, Haley glanced over her shoulder. She sighed with relief. "He's gone," she said. "Gee, why do boys have to be so gross and such pests?"

"I don't know," said Anna. "Maybe they're just born that way and can't help it. Or, maybe not all of them are as bad as Scott," she added thoughtfully. "Don't you think there must be some boys who are normal?"

"Hah! Get serious!" exclaimed Haley. "It's just a fact. All boys definitely are impossible. Trust me."

"Yeah," said Anna. "You're probably right."

Suddenly, the girls heard a car horn beeping behind them. They stopped walking and quickly turned around to see who it was.

"It's Lauren!" exclaimed Haley. She watched as her older sister pulled her little blue car over to the side of the road.

"Do you guys want a ride home?" asked Lauren through the open window.

"Sure!" Haley scrambled into the front seat,

while Anna climbed into the back. There were fashion magazines and soda pop cans scattered on the back seat and the floor.

"Wow!" sighed Anna as she pushed the pile aside. "It must be neat to have an older sister who can drive."

"Yeah. It can be fun," agreed Haley. She grinned and stared across the seat at Lauren. Black curls tumbled over Lauren's shoulders. Pink nail polish gleamed from her fingernails, which were carefully gripping the steering wheel.

As Haley watched Lauren pull the car slowly away from the curb, she thought about the way people compared her with Lauren. People often said how much they look alike. They both have black, curly hair. But Lauren's hair is much longer. And they both have blue eyes, but Lauren wears makeup on hers because she thinks it makes her look prettier and *older.*

"Look!" exclaimed Anna. "There's Scott again."

Haley looked out the window and saw Scott walking alone along the sidewalk.

"Do you want to give him a ride, too?" asked Lauren, slowing the car.

"No-o-o-o-o!" Haley and Anna both shouted at the same time.

Scott looked at their car. He grinned from ear to ear when he saw Haley peering at him through the car window.

"Oh, how gross," said Haley. She stuck her tongue out at him. Scott made a monkey face back at her.

Lauren turned a corner, and soon Scott was out of sight.

Haley leaned toward Lauren. She frowned for a moment. Then she said, "Lauren, can I ask you a question about boys?"

"Sure," said Lauren. "But I might not have the answer for you. I'm not exactly an expert on the subject, you know."

Haley squirmed in her seat. "But you're 17," she said. "You've dated, and you know things about *everything*."

"I don't know as much as you think I do," said Lauren, pressing her lips together in thought. "What's your question?" she asked.

Haley spoke the words slowly. "What makes boys so weird?"

"Yeah," said Anna. She leaned forward and folded her arms over the top of the seat back. "Why do boys always act like geeks all the time?"

Lauren grinned, and then she laughed. "Things will change when you get older," she promised. "You can count on it."

"Do boys quit being so goofy?" asked Haley. Her blue eyes stared up at her sister.

Lauren thought for a moment. "No," she said, hesitantly. "I don't think boys ever stop acting goofy. When they get older, they just act goofy in a different way." Lauren smiled to herself.

"Yuck!" exclaimed Haley. She squeezed her nose with her thumb and finger. "P.U. on boys," she said.

"P.U.," Anna agreed, lightly pinching her own nose. "Boys stink!"

"You can say that again," said Haley. She watched out the car window at the passing houses and trees. After awhile, she leaned her head back against the seat and said, "I swear I'll *never* like boys."

"Me either," added Anna, shaking her head from side to side for emphasis.

Haley turned excitedly to her sister. "I have an idea!" she announced. "Let's promise to be friends forever. Okay?"

"That's easy," said Anna. "Friends forever!"

"Forever," agreed Lauren with a chuckle. She reached across the seat and slid an arm around Haley's shoulder. "Yes, we'll be sisters and friends forever," she announced, giving her little sister a warm smile.

Haley heaved a sigh of relief. She reminded herself how lucky she was to have an older sister like Lauren, and a friend like Anna.

Anna has been her best friend ever since Anna and her family moved from Texas to Parkland, Kansas, two years ago.

Haley thought to herself how wonderful the future would be if just she, Anna, and Lauren were friends. Maybe the three of them could live together someday, and they could have 100 dogs and cats to love. And they could have horses roaming freely around the backyard. *Boy, would that be fun!* Haley thought.

Lauren pulled her car into their driveway beside their parents' car. Anna hopped out of the backseat. "Thanks for the ride. I'll walk home from here," she said. "It's just down the road."

"Wait!" called Haley. "Why don't you stay for supper tonight? Maybe Lauren could even take us for hamburgers. Would you, Lauren? Please? We could have hamburgers, fries, and strawberry shakes. Please?"

"Sure," said Lauren easily. "I'll take you both if Mom and Dad say it's okay."

Haley ran into the house, and Anna followed closely behind. She found her mom in the kitchen. There were boxes and tubes of makeup all over the table. Her mom was sorting orders and putting eyeliner, mascara, face powder, blush, eye shadow, and creams into little white bags. All the colors of the rainbow peered out from the tubes and boxes of makeup.

Haley picked up a tube of purple lipstick. "Does anyone really wear this stuff, Mom?" she asked.

Mrs. Boster grinned a little tiredly. "You'd be surprised," she said. "I've been selling a lot of this color lately." Haley noticed a cluster of white paper bags on the kitchen counter. "Are those ready to be delivered?" she asked.

Mrs. Boster nodded her head. "Business is pretty good these days," she said. "I've got eight deliveries to make this evening. I never thought when I started selling Angel Cosmetics that sales would be so good. Even Dad admits he's surprised at how much I've sold."

Haley gave Anna a big grin, signaling that the time was right to ask about supper. Then, turning back to her mother, she said, "Well, since you seem to be pretty busy tonight, can Lauren take Anna and me out for hamburgers?"

"Sure," said Mrs. Boster. "If it's okay with Lauren."

Just then, Lauren walked into the room. She glanced at the jumble of makeup, and then walked over to start inspecting for herself. She picked up a tube of lipstick and removed the cap. Then she twisted the tube, and a coral shade of lipstick appeared at the end of the tube. "Mmmmmm," she said. "This is a great color, Mom. Do you mind if I buy this one?"

When her mom agreed, Lauren reached into her purse to get some money. She handed her mother two slightly crumpled dollar bills.

"Two bucks!" shouted Haley. "You pay two bucks for that little thing? For two dollars, you could get a four- dip ice cream cone. You could get a cheeseburger and small fries. You could even get a bunch of rubber spiders and lizards."

Just then, the phone rang. Haley hurried to answer it. "Hello?" she said. She listened to the voice on the other end for a moment. Then she handed the receiver to Lauren. "It's for you. It's a boy," Haley said, sticking out her tongue. "Yuck!"

Haley did not want to hear their conversation, so she trekked up the stairs to her bedroom. Anna followed closely behind. Falling across her bed, Haley said, "Maybe we can talk Lauren into taking us out for ice cream after dinner. We could go to the Dairy Freeze. All the fun kids hang out there."

Anna said, "Yeah, let's tell her about the flavors of ice cream to make her hungry. Then she'll take us. My favorite flavor is mint chocolate chip. If I had to eat one thing for the rest of my life, that's what it would be."

There was a knock on Haley's door. "Come in," said Haley. She sat up on the edge of her bed, and swung her legs around so they were on the floor.

Lauren opened the door and stepped hesitantly into the room. She looked from Haley to Anna. Then with a shrug of her shoulders, she said, "I'm really sorry, guys. But we'll have to go for hamburgers another night, okay?"

Haley jumped to her feet. "Why?" she asked.

Lauren smiled, coral lipstick framing her even white teeth. "I've got a date!" she announced cheerfully.

"You mean you're going out with a *boy?*" Haley demanded in complete disbelief.

"Of course, with a boy, silly," Lauren replied. "His name is Gary Aberdeen," she added with a sigh. "I didn't even think he knew I was alive. He's so cute, and he seems smart *and nice.* He graduated this year, so he's a year older than me. I don't know him very well— *yet.* Boy, I'll really have something to write

19

in my diary tonight. I am so excited but I'm nervous, too." Lauren smiled. But Haley didn't return her excitement.

Haley sat down on the edge of her bed. She pursed her lips together in disappointment.

Lauren crossed the room and sat beside her. "I'm sorry," she said. "I know how much you both wanted to go tonight. But I promise that I'll make it up to you. We'll go out for hamburgers real soon." With that, she stood up and left the room.

Haley and Anna looked at each other in disappointment and disgust.

"Boys!" exclaimed Anna.

"Yeah. See, I told you they always ruin *everything*," growled Haley.

Two

HALEY and Anna both lay sprawled on the grass in Haley's front yard. The grass tickled the back of Haley's legs. Pointing at a cloud formation overhead, she said, "That one over there looks just like Gary Aberdeen. See how the cloud sticks out. It looks just like his ears and his feet because they're weird and too big. He's such a jerk. I don't know why Lauren likes him so much."

Anna sat up and brushed an ant off of her knee. "Does she see him a lot?" she asked.

Haley made a whinnying sound through her lips, which sounded a little like a horse. "They've been together *every day* for the last week. I just can't stand it. He picks her up every night after dinner. It's just gross."

Anna nodded her head in sympathy. "Where is Lauren now?" she asked.

Haley sat up and pulled bits of grass from her dark curls. "Oh, she's here right now. She's probably inside writing in her diary," she moaned. "She's always either with Gary, or else she's writing in her diary. That's about all she does. I never get to be with her anymore."

A car pulled into the driveway, and Mrs. Boster got out. She took an empty box from the backseat. Smiling at the girls, she said, "There. I've made my last cosmetics delivery for the day." Then noticing their expressions, she added, "Hey, what's wrong with you two?"

"There's nothing to do," Haley said sadly. "Lauren never does stuff with us anymore. She's always *too busy*." Haley wrinkled her nose and added "with Gary" as if there was a gross smell in the air.

"I think Gary's a nice young man," said Mrs.

Boster in his defense. "Come on inside. Let's make some lemonade."

Haley and Anna followed her into the house. Mrs. Boster opened a can of lemonade while Anna measured the correct amount of water. Haley stirred it all together in a big glass pitcher, and then she poured three tall glasses. They all sat around the the kitchen table.

"Okay, so what's the problem?" asked Mrs. Boster. "Summer vacation has just started, and both of you are bored already?" A little smile tugged at the corners of Mrs. Boster's mouth.

Haley leaned her elbow onto the table and rested her head in her hand. "Lauren's always with Gary," she complained. "She used to do things with us and take us places, but now she's forgotten about us."

"So, why don't you think about doing something else?" asked Mrs. Boster. "You girls can have fun without Lauren, can't you? After all, Lauren's growing up. She's developing new

23

interests. You will too someday."

"But why, Mom?" asked Haley. She turned her blue eyes up to her mother.

Mrs. Boster just sighed in response. "You'll find out one of these days," she said.

"You don't mean *boys*, do you?" Haley shook her head vigorously. "Forget it," she said. "We'll *never* like boys!"

"That's right, Mrs. Boster," agreed Anna, nodding her head. "Haley and I are going to stay exactly the way we are right now. We're not going to be like Lauren and like *them*."

"Great," said Mrs. Boster, trying to hide her amusement. "That means we'll save a lot of money on new clothes and shoes then, won't we?"

Haley took a long drink of her lemonade. It tasted great on a hot June afternoon like today.

Mrs. Boster stood up from the table. She said, "You girls need to get your minds on something fun. Why don't you think about summer camp? You two are planning to share a cabin, aren't you? Well, I'm sure you can have a lot of fun thinking about what you're going to do there. You'll have two whole weeks together at Hawthorne Ridge Camp."

Haley's face brightened at the thought. But then she frowned again, realizing that she still had two weeks to wait. "But, Mom, what are we going to do for two weeks?" she groaned.

"Hmm." Mrs. Boster put her hand on her hip while she thought about Haley's question. Then she clapped her hands, and broke into a big smile. "I've got a great idea!" she cried, her face brightening. "Why don't you girls practice your camping skills? You can sleep out in the backyard tonight. Then you'll be expert campers by the time you go off to camp."

Haley jumped up out of her chair. She threw her arms around her mother's waist and gave her a big hug. "That's a great idea, Mom. It'll be so much fun! Can we use Dad's camping equipment?"

"Sure," said Mrs. Boster. "It's out in the

garage somewhere."

Anna called her mother to get permission to sleep over. Then she and Haley raced to the garage where they pulled a bundled up tent down from a lower shelf. Right behind the sleeping bag, they found a canteen, binoculars, a flashlight, a compass, little tin plates, and two sleeping bags.

"This stuff is really great," said Anna. "I didn't know your Dad had all this stuff around here."

"Oh, sure," said Haley. "Dad and Mom used to go camping together a lot, especially when they were younger."

Haley and Anna carried the camping equipment out into the Bosters' backyard. After a few failed attempts, they set the tent up under a large, oak tree. Using an oversized hammer, Haley pounded the stakes into the ground. A cord ran from the tent walls to the stakes, pulling the walls out at an angle. Two poles, one at the front and one at the back, held the tent roof up off the ground. Inside, the tent was actually cozy and cool.

Haley wiped drops of sweat from her forehead. She stood back and inspected the tent. "It looks really good," she said approvingly.

She and Anna crawled into the tent and sat cross-legged on the ground. The tops of their heads brushed the tent's ceiling.

"It's great," said Anna. She smoothed the bumps out of the canvas floor.

Haley arranged the canteen and plates together in a row. Then she held the binoculars up to her eyes. "Cool," she said. "I can see way into the distance." She handed the binoculars to Anna.

The rest of the afternoon was spent running in and out of the house, carrying things to the tent.

"We'll definitely want these comic books," said Haley.

"Right. And don't forget the potato chips," said Anna. "We might want to have snacks to eat later, and chips are the *best.*"

"And we'll need squirt guns," said Haley. "In case any dogs try to get into our tent, we'll be ready to shoot them with water."

* * * * *

It was 6:00 when Mr. Boster came home from work that day. Haley heard his car door slam shut. "Dad! Will you come here?"

Mr. Boster walked around the house into the backyard. He smiled when he saw Haley and Anna by the tent. He set his briefcase down on the back porch, then he strolled over to the tent. "Wow!" he cried. "This is all of my old camping gear. It's been such a long time since your mom and I have used this stuff. What are you girls up to with it?"

"We're practicing for summer camp," Haley explained. "Mom said it'd be okay if we sleep out here tonight."

Mr. Boster bent over, peering into the tent.

"Where are you going to sleep?" he asked. "It doesn't look to me like there's much room in there."

Haley glanced back into the tent at the binoculars, sleeping bags, comic books, flashlights, tin dishes, bag of potato chips, and squirt guns. "Oh, Dad," she said. "What do you mean? There's plenty of room."

Mr. Boster said, "Okay, if that's the way you want it. I'm glad someone's getting some use out of this old stuff." He turned and walked across the yard to the house.

Haley watched through the kitchen window as her mom and dad kissed. Then Mrs. Boster appeared at the back door. "Dinner's ready!" she called.

Haley and Anna ran into the house. Haley saw that the dining room table was set for four people, meaning Lauren must be going out *again*. At that moment, Lauren walked into the room in her bathrobe.

"Mom, do you have any dark blue mascara

that I can use?" she asked.

"Sure, it's in my makeup bag," said Mrs. Boster.

Lauren turned around and left the room. Mr. and Mrs. Boster, Haley, and Anna sat down at the table.

"Isn't Lauren going to eat with us?" asked Haley.

"No," explained Mrs. Boster. "Lauren's going out to dinner with Gary tonight."

"Oh brother," huffed Haley with a toss of her head. "I should've known."

Just as they finished their salads, the doorbell rang. Haley jumped up from the table and pulled the front door open to find a young man standing there. He was tall with short, brown hair and brown eyes.

"Oh," said Haley, with clear disappointment. "It's only you."

"Hello, Gary," called out Mr. Boster, as he got up from the table and walked toward the door. "Come on in. It's nice to see you again.

Lauren will be ready in just a minute."

Haley glared at Gary as he came into the house. "Hello, Mrs. Boster," Gary said. "Please go on eating. I don't want to interrupt your dinner."

It's too late for that, Haley thought to herself. *You've already interrupted dinner and everything else.*

Lauren flounced into the room, looking pretty and smelling like fresh lilacs. She smiled shyly at Gary. "Hi," she said. "I'm ready."

"You look nice," said Gary.

Haley noted that Lauren was wearing more makeup these days. That night she wore pink lipstick, blue eye shadow, and matching mascara that accented her crystal blue eyes. Her hair looked curlier than ever, falling down over her shoulders. She wore a white skirt, and her feet were strapped into petite white sandals.

As Lauren walked over to stand by Gary,

Haley wrinkled her nose to signal her disgust.

"Bye, everyone!" called Lauren as she and Gary walked out the front door and down the porch steps. Haley let herself watch until Gary helped Lauren into the passenger's seat of his snazzy car. Then she couldn't stand it and returned to her place at the table.

Mr. and Mrs. Boster waved good-bye. Haley sat and stared at her empty plate. Anna sat patiently in her place, waiting for dinner to be served.

"Mom," said Haley. "Can Anna and I eat outside in the tent?"

Mrs. Boster sighed understandingly. "All right," she said as she exchanged concerned glances with her husband.

"Why don't you use your camping dishes?" Mr. Boster suggested.

It seemed like a good idea to Haley and Anna. They got their tin plates and cups from the tent. Then they helped themselves to a supper of potato salad, green beans, fried chicken, and rolls. Haley and Anna heaped the food onto their plates, and then they returned to their tent.

Inside, they sat cross-legged and ate their dinner.

"This is cool," said Haley. "It's almost like real camping."

Anna brushed a fly off of her potato salad. "Yeah," she said. "This is neat."

When dinner was over, the girls washed their dishes with the garden hose. The sun set, and soon it grew dim inside the tent. Haley and Anna went into the house to change into their pajamas. But to be safe, they kept running shoes on their feet.

"You never know when you're going to have to run away from a bear," explained Haley when she saw her father's curious glance.

"Kansas isn't too well-known for its large bear population," said Mr. Boster. "But I guess it's better to be prepared for anything," he added with a wink.

Haley and Anna walked through the kitchen, grabbed a few more snacks, and headed back into the yard. They walked carefully to the tent to avoid stepping on anything. Once inside, they each lay down on their sleeping bag. A crunching noise came from somewhere in the back of the tent.

"Oops!" said Anna. "I put my foot in the bag of potato chips."

Haley lay on her back with her arms crossed under her head. Looking out from the tent's opening she saw the dark shape of the huge oak tree stretching over them. The twigs and branches looked a little like scary fingers and arms spreading out into the night sky.

"What would you do if you were in a tent under a tree, and there was a mountain lion in the tree?" asked Haley. "And what if he hadn't eaten in a *week*?" she added eerily.

Anna shivered in the sleeping bag next to Haley. "I'd move my tent," said Anna. "What would *you* do if a crazy man escaped from prison and found you all alone in your tent? And what if he had a *hook?*"

"Whoa!" exclaimed Haley, turning onto her stomach. "I guess that's why you should sleep with running shoes on."

As the night grew darker, Haley and Anna discussed ghosts, vampires, escaped convicts, aliens from outer space, and giant, killer ants—the kind that eat you to pieces.

A sudden *plop* sounded on the roof of their tent just as Anna was describing what killer ants can do.

"Eeek!" Haley and Anna sat up with a shriek. Haley felt her heart pounding hard inside her chest.

Then logic returned, and she calmed down. "It was just an acorn," she said reasonably. "Maybe it wasn't such a great idea putting our tent underneath a tree."

"I thought for a minute it was a giant killer ant getting ready to attack us," said Anna with a nervous laugh.

"Gee," said Haley, lying back down. "It must be late. But I'm not sleepy yet."

"I'm not either," said Anna. "Maybe we should quit talking about monsters and stuff."

"Listen!" said Haley, sitting up once again.

The two girls listened as the sound of a car pulling up in front of the Boster house grew louder.

"Come on," whispered Haley. "Let's check it out!"

Flicking on their flashlights, the girls crawled out from the tent and ran through the yard. They crept carefully along the side of the house. They shut off their flashlights, and knelt behind a bush and waited.

"Look. It's Gary and Lauren!" whispered Haley. She frowned to herself in the dark.

Haley watched through the leaves as Gary opened the car door for Lauren. Their voices were soft and faraway. Haley strained to hear what they were saying. She crept a little closer, but she shielded herself behind the bush. She watched as Gary and Lauren walked together to the front door.

"They're holding hands," whispered Anna.

Haley stared in shock as her older sister stood on her tiptoes. Gary looked at her adoringly, and their faces came together in a quick kiss beneath the porch light. "How gross!" Haley whispered behind the bush. "I think I'm going to be sick!"

The front door opened, and Lauren disappeared into the house. Gary walked back to the car.

"We should have brought our squirt guns," said Haley, regretfully.

Gary started the car's engine. The headlights came on, and soon he had driven out of sight.

Haley and Anna sat behind the bush in stunned silence. At last Anna said, "Gee, Haley. It looks like your sister really likes this guy."

"Things are worse than I thought," Haley agreed. "If Lauren really likes Gary, then I'll

never see her anymore."

A lump rose in Haley's throat. She felt hot tears rush into her eyes. "I wonder if Lauren likes Gary more than she likes me," she said, feeling rejected and abandoned.

Slowly, the girls retraced their steps through the darkness. They climbed into their tent. Haley watched the back of her house and saw Lauren's light glowing from her bedroom window.

"She's probably writing in her diary," she said, sadly. "She'll probably write about kissing Gary. I hate it."

"Let's not talk about kissing anymore," said Anna. "I might get sick."

"What am I going to do?" asked Haley, staring up at the tent ceiling. "I've got to do something so that Lauren won't like Gary anymore."

Anna rolled over in her sleeping bag. "Maybe we could tell Lauren that Gary is already married," she suggested. "Or maybe we could tell her that he has a terrible disease, and if she keeps kissing him, her hair will fall out."

"Why do boys have to ruin everything?" asked Haley angrily.

"I don't know," said Anna. "But if you ask me, we girls have to stick together."

Suddenly, Haley had an idea. "Hey, I know what we can do!" she exclaimed. "You and I can have a club. We'll call it The Boy Busters Club! We'll take an oath that we'll never like boys, and we'll never wear makeup and all that yucky stuff to impress them."

"No problem," said Anna. She reached for the bag of potato chips and munched on some chips. Passing the bag to Haley, she said, "What else will we do in our club?"

Haley put her hand over her heart. "We'll pledge that we'll never become wimps," she said thoughtfully. "We'll always play kickball, softball, and basketball. We'll always skateboard, swim, run, and do all the fun things

40

that boys and girls do. But we won't do them with boys."

"This sounds like fun," said Anna.

Haley smiled happily into the dark. "And you know what else?" she asked.

"What?" asked Anna.

"The main purpose of The Boy Busters Club is to help Lauren break up with Gary. Then she can take us out for hamburgers and drive us around like she used to."

Haley snuggled her cheek against her pillow. Suddenly, everything didn't seem so awful or impossible. As she fell asleep, she said to herself, *just be patient, because pretty soon Lauren will be free. Then the three of us can have lots of fun together again. Everything will be great—as soon as Gary is out of the picture!*

Three

H ALEY and Anna woke up early the next morning feeling refreshed. They brushed potato chip and cookie crumbs out of their tent, and then they made their way to the house for breakfast. Lauren was seated at the kitchen table with her parents.

As Haley walked into the kitchen, she heard her sister say, "Oh Mom! You should've seen the restaurant! The waiters wore white gloves. There were flowers on every table. There was even a man playing guitar and singing love songs. It was wonderful!"

"It just sounds like a bunch of mush to me," Haley whispered from the side of her mouth. Anna nodded her agreement.

43

"Good morning, campers," Mr. Boster greeted them. "I hope the mosquitoes didn't eat you alive last night." Haley could tell it meant a lot to him that they had dug out his old camping gear and were enjoying the outdoors.

"They weren't too bad," Haley said, scratching at a cluster of red bumps on her arm.

Mr. Boster stood up from the table. He glanced at his wristwatch. "I'd better get moving," he said, "or else I'll be late for work." He kissed Mrs. Boster quickly, and then hurried out the door. Moments later, Haley heard the hum of his car's engine as he backed down the driveway.

Lauren reached out and patted Haley on the shoulder. "How's it going, you two?" she asked cheerfully.

Haley returned her sister's smile. It was nice just to be with her, sitting at the breakfast table together. Haley spooned some scrambled eggs onto her plate. Then slowly, she asked, "Lauren, what do you really know about Gary? I mean, are you sure you should see him again? You know, he could have a disease that you don't know about."

Lauren stared at Haley for a moment. Then she giggled. "Oh, Haley," she said. "What are you talking about?"

Haley glanced at Anna for support. Anna nodded her head as if to say, "Go ahead. Tell her."

"Well," Haley said. "I hate to be the one to tell you, but you know Gary might live in a cave."

Lauren laughed loudly. Mrs. Boster said, "Haley, I think that sleeping outside is getting your imagination too worked up."

Haley shook her head. "No," she insisted. "It's just that Lauren hardly even knows him. He might be a maniac or something."

Lauren reached across the table to touch Haley lightly on the cheek. "Don't worry," Lauren said. "Gary's a really nice guy. He's not a maniac, and he doesn't live in a cave. He lives with his parents on Mulberry Street. I promise you, Haley. He's okay, really."

Haley buttered a piece of toast. She gazed across the table at her sister. Lauren smiled quietly as if she was thinking of something wonderful. Haley frowned. *Lauren used to share all her secrets with me,* she thought. *But she never tells me anything anymore. Now that she likes Gary, she probably doesn't like me.*

Haley dropped her fork to the table with a clatter. "I know!" she said suddenly. "Why don't you take me and Anna to the mall today? We could check out the toy store and go see a movie."

As soon as Haley saw the look on Lauren's face, she knew Lauren had other plans—plans that probably involved *him.* Lauren looked apologetic. "I'm sorry," she said. "Gary's coming over in a little while. He's taking me to meet his aunt and uncle today. They live way out in the country."

Haley didn't say a word. She just looked down at her plate and stuffed the last piece of toast into her mouth. Then she and Anna went back to her bedroom to change into T-shirts and shorts.

Haley checked to be sure the bedroom door was closed tightly. Then she whispered to Anna, "It looks like we're going to have to do some spying."

"What do you mean?" asked Anna, lacing up her shoe.

Haley put her hands on her hips. "If we're going to find out anything bad about Gary, we're going to have to watch him. I'll even talk to him if I have to. It's the only way to find out some bad stuff, so Lauren won't have to see him anymore. She'll thank us for filling her in."

Haley gritted her teeth together. She kicked at a Nerf ball on the floor. "I wish that was Gary," she said. "I just don't know how

Lauren can stand kissing and all that gross mushy stuff."

"Yeck!" exclaimed Anna. "Long live the Boy Busters Club!"

Haley and Anna shook hands as if to seal that thought. Haley thought about how great it would be in two weeks when she and Anna left for camp. There'd be no kissing and mushy stuff there—just some great swimming, hiking, sports, and games. They planned to share a cabin. Camp would be heaven! They also would get to enjoy fishing, crafts, and sitting around the camp fire singing corny songs. Maybe this year she'd even learn how to pitch a softball.

Haley sighed. Boy, two weeks sure seemed like a long time to wait for camp. She jumped when she heard the sound of a car door slamming. Running to her window, Haley peered out. "It's only Gary," she growled. She stared at him as he walked up the front walk. "Anna, look how big his ears are," Haley complained.

48

"And his hair's way too short."

"I don't like his pants either," said Anna.

Glancing up at the window, Gary smiled and waved. Haley jumped back and let the curtain fall into place.

"Rats!" she gasped. "He saw us looking at him."

The doorbell rang. "Now's the time to put our plan into action," said Haley.

"What plan?" asked Anna.

"Spying," said Haley. "Come on. Follow me."

The two girls left the bedroom, and went downstairs to answer the door. "Hi, Gary," Haley said. "Come on in."

"Hi, Haley. Hi, Anna." Gary walked into the living room and sat in the easy chair. "It's a great day out there," he said, smiling. Haley inspected Gary from head to toe. She stared at him. *I think my sister should go out with someone better looking,* she thought.

Gary shifted uneasily in his seat. "Is Lauren ready yet?" he asked.

"Not quite," said Haley. "She's probably curling her eyebrows or something."

Gary looked surprised at that image. He smiled. Haley walked over to where he sat, leaned close to him, and asked, "Do you mind if I ask you a question?"

"Uh, no. What would you like to know, Haley?" asked Gary.

Haley cleared her throat, and then glanced sideways at Anna. Looking back at Gary, she asked, "Have you ever been in prison?"

"What?" Gary sat up straighter. Right then, Lauren came into the room. Again, Haley breathed in the sweet scent of lilacs. Lauren looked as lovely as ever in lemon yellow shorts and a white, knit top. She sat down beside Gary on the couch.

Gary looked nervously away from Haley. He smiled at Lauren. "Aunt Cheryl and Uncle Nick are looking forward to meeting you," he said. "I think you'll like them. And I know they'll definitely like you."

Haley noticed that Lauren seemed too embarrassed to say anything. It was a sappy,
mushy, romantic kind of embarrassed. Haley
and Anna crossed their eyes at each other.

They're not even talking, Haley thought.
They just stare at each other like monkeys.
Haley was determined to get something out of
Gary before they left. "Gary," she said. "Do
you have any deep, dark secrets that we don't
know about?"

Lauren jumped up from the couch. "Haley!"
she exclaimed. "What a rude question!"

Haley heard the anger in her sister's voice,
and she felt bad. "I'm sorry," she said, as she
silently planned what to ask him next time.

Gary gave a half smile. "Yeah, sure, I've got
a few secrets," he said. "But I don't think
they're too deep or too dark."

Lauren stared down at Haley. "I'm surprised at you, Haley," she said softly. Haley
felt that her sister was disappointed in her,
and that did make her feel bad.

"Come on, Gary," said Lauren. "Let's go outside. We can leave as soon as Mom gets home. She's out making a few cosmetics deliveries."

Lauren and Gary opened the screen door and went out to sit on the new porch swing. "I don't think they want to be with us," said Anna.

"We didn't find out anything bad about him," said Haley. "Let's watch them through the window."

Climbing up sneakily behind the sofa and peering through the thin curtains, the girls craned their necks so that they could see Lauren and Gary sitting together on the front porch.

"Look!" cried Anna. "There's something square in his back pocket. Ooh, they must be cigarettes! Lauren wouldn't go out with him if she found out about that."

Haley looked more closely. "Nah," she said. "That's just his wallet. Hey, but look in his other pocket," exclaimed Haley, a sudden glimmer of hope appearing. "It looks like a knife! I wonder if Lauren knows about that!"

Gary reached into his back pocket and pulled out a pack of gum. He offered a piece to Lauren.

"Oh, shoot!" said Haley. "I guess it wasn't a knife, after all."

As Haley leaned further toward the window, she lost her grip on the windowsill, and her head banged against the glass. Gary and Lauren looked up in alarm. Lauren frowned when she realized who it was.

Haley and Anna fell away from the window onto the sofa. Dropping to their knees on the floor, they crawled toward the front door.

"We can get a good view from the door," whispered Haley. Lauren's voice came floating in. "Haley! You better quit spying on me, or you're going to be in serious trouble when Mom gets home. I mean it!"

Haley and Anna stopped in mid-crawl. As

they knelt on the floor wondering what to do, Mrs. Boster pulled into the driveway. Haley heard Lauren yell good-bye to her. At the sound of Gary's engine, Haley and Anna raced to the door to watch them leave.

As Mrs. Boster walked into the house, Haley ran over to her. "Mom!" she squealed. "Did you see the way Gary was driving? He was going way too fast! Lauren shouldn't be dating such a crazy driver, should she?"

Mrs. Boster looked curiously down at Haley. "I saw them leave, Haley," she said, "and his driving looked okay to me."

Feeling hopeless, Haley and Anna returned to Boy Busters' headquarters in the backyard tent. A bright blue sky stretched overhead. Birds sung from the large oak above the tent. But Haley was feeling miserable.

"What'll we do now?" asked Anna. "How will we ever find out any bad secrets about Gary?"

Haley thought and thought. She flipped

through a comic book for a few moments, and then threw it into the back of the tent. With a grim look on her face, she said, "I've got another plan."

"What?" asked Anna.

Haley gritted her teeth. "It calls for more dangerous spy work," she said. "Are you game?"

"Sure," said Anna. "I'm game."

"Good," said Haley. She pointed up to Lauren's bedroom window. "We'll find some answers for sure in there," she said, mysteriously.

Anna looked puzzled.

"Lauren's diary!" gushed Haley. "All her deepest, darkest secrets are in there. I'll bet she wrote about Gary. We can find out if she really likes him. And maybe we can find out some bad stuff about him."

Anna made an okay sign with her fingers. "Let's go, Sherlock," she said.

Mrs. Boster was at the kitchen table sorting through makeup orders when Haley and Anna walked in. Haley struggled not to let the excitement show in her face. Once out of the kitchen, she and Anna raced upstairs. Stopping for a moment to listen, Haley quietly turned the knob on her sister's bedroom door.

Pushing the door open, Haley and Anna stepped into Lauren's room. A blue, ruffled spread was pulled up neatly over the bed. There were bookshelves and a dresser covered with crystal bottles, lipstick tubes, and boxes of earrings. A white, lace doily decorated a bedside table

"I know that she keeps her diary in her dresser drawer," said Haley in a hushed voice.

Creeping across the blue carpet, Haley's footsteps didn't make a sound. She silently opened the dresser drawer, and reached under a pile of silk scarves until she felt a book beneath her fingertips. Pulling it out, she said excitedly, "This is it!"

Haley and Anna stared at the little pink

and blue book with the gold clasp on its side. There was a big lock on the clasp, but it didn't look used much.

"What if it's locked?" asked Anna worriedly.

Haley looked upset, too—until she gave the lock a try, and it opened easily. Flipping rapidly through the pages, Haley saw that the book was covered with neat, little writing. Turning to the latest entry, Haley quickly read for highlights and then frowned.

"Gee," said Haley, with a pout. "She mentions Gary about a hundred times. She doesn't even mention me *once.*"

Haley flipped through pages as Anna stood beside her patiently waiting for any news.

"What are you doing in my room?" came a loud boom from behind them.

Haley and Anna shrieked at the sound of Lauren's angry voice. Haley turned around guiltily to find her sister standing in the doorway. *And, boy, did Lauren look mad.*

Four

"LAUREN! What are you doing here?" asked Haley.

Lauren walked across the room past Anna, and plucked the diary from Haley's hands. "What am *I* doing here? What are *you two* doing with my diary? That's private. I forgot my purse and had to come back for it. Obviously, it's a good thing I did," said Lauren. She reached angrily into her closet and took a purse from the top shelf.

Haley didn't know what to say. She stood silently.

"I'm very disappointed in you, Haley," said Lauren. "And I'm disappointed in you, too, Anna," she added.

Anna looked down at the blue carpet.

"I thought that I could trust you," said Lauren, looking back at Haley. "I never thought I'd catch you snooping around my room."

I never thought you would either, Haley thought regretfully.

"You are not allowed in my room without my permission," said Lauren. "And if I ever, I mean *ever,* catch you reading my diary again, I'll...I'll...."

"What's all the fuss about?" Mrs. Boster asked as she entered the bedroom.

Oh no, Haley thought. *Now I'm really going to get in trouble!*

Lauren waved the diary high in the air. "I caught Haley in here reading my diary," she exclaimed. "Can you believe it?"

Haley felt like crawling under the bed when she saw the expression on her mother's face.

"Haley Sue Boster!" cried Mrs. Boster. "What's gotten into you lately? You know your sister's diary is private. You're not a little girl anymore. You know better than that."

"Yes, ma'am," said Haley in a voice as timid as a mouse's.

"And you know you're not allowed in your sister's room without her permission, don't you?"

"Yes, ma'am," Haley said again. She shifted uneasily on her feet. Glancing sideways at Anna, she saw that Anna's chin was trembling.

Haley turned to her sister. "I'm sorry," she said.

"Don't do it again," Lauren said. "I mean it." Looking at her new, red watch, an early birthday present from Gary, she said, "Oh no! Gary and I are going to be late. I've got to go." Then she darted from the room. Haley heard her sister's feet patter down the stairs, the front door being opened, and soon the familiar sound of Gary's car engine.

Haley and Anna left the bedroom. Mrs. Boster closed the door behind them. "I'm surprised at you, Haley," said Mrs. Boster, shaking her head.

I seem to be surprising a lot of people these days, Haley thought. *It seems like someone's always mad at me about something. I spend more time in trouble than out of trouble.*

Haley and Anna walked down the stairs and through the kitchen. They returned to their headquarters in the backyard.

Haley flopped down on her sleeping bag. "It seems like this is the only place where no one yells at me," she said.

Anna crawled into the tent. "Yeah," she agreed. "I can't believe Lauren forgot her purse. What luck."

Haley made a fist and banged it against the tent's canvas floor. "Everything was okay until Gary came along," she moaned. "Lauren used to *like* me. Now she *hates* me."

"And she used to take us out for ice cream," said Anna.

"And she used to drive us around town,"

added Haley. "We used to play checkers after dinner. And we used to sing stupid stuff together when we cleared off the dinner table."

Haley leaned her chin onto her fist. She watched as an ant struggled to carry a potato chip crumb across the tent floor.

"I've just got to think of a way to break up Lauren and Gary," she growled. "After all, that's the main goal of The Boy Busters Club."

Anna reached from the tent into the yard and picked a blade of grass. She chewed on its pointed green tip.

"Maybe we could send Gary a letter telling him he got a job in Alaska," said Haley. Her eyebrows shot up at the idea.

"Nah," said Anna. "He'd know it was fake for sure. Hmm. Maybe you could tell Lauren that Gary is an alien from outer space."

Haley looked at her friend and rolled her eyes. With a shake of her head, she said, "Lauren would never fall for that."

Haley flipped over onto her back. Beads of

sweat trickled from her scalp into her ears. "Boy, it's hot in here," she said.

Haley snapped her fingers. "I've got it!" she said. "If we can find a beautiful girl Gary's age and introduce him to her, then he'll drop Lauren like a hot potato."

"Do you know any beautiful girls Gary's age?" asked Anna.

"No," Haley admitted.

Mrs. Boster's voice came from the back porch. "Anna!" she called. "Your mother just phoned. She wants you to come home."

Anna crawled quickly out of the tent. "Oops!" she said. "I forgot that I was supposed to be home early. See you later, Haley." Racing across the lawn, she disappeared around the corner of the house.

Haley reached for a comic book. But it was one she'd read a hundred times. She tossed it into the back of the tent where it landed on top of some half-melted chocolate bars. She rolled onto her side, and a drop of sweat fell from her face to the ground.

I'll just stay out here in the tent, she told herself. *Every time I leave the tent I get into trouble, anyway. Mom's mad at me. Lauren's mad at me. Dad will be mad when Mom tells him about the diary. Everybody hates me. They'll probably all be glad when I go off to Hawthorne Ridge. Then they'll be rid of me for two whole weeks.*

The thought of camp cheered her up a little. Haley imagined diving into the camp lake and swimming to the platform several feet out into the water. Kids always jumped up onto the platform and dove off. She also pictured herself sitting by a camp fire with soft marshmallows toasting on a stick. *And Anna would be there, the only person in the world who wasn't mad at me,* Haley thought.

By late afternoon, the chocolate bars in the tent had melted. Haley carried the soggy wrappers into the house where she put the limp chocolate bars in the refrigerator. Her mother sat at the table reading through cosmetics order forms.

Haley looked carefully at her mother to see if she was still mad at her. But Mrs. Boster smiled and said, "There's lemonade in the fridge, dear."

Haley poured herself a big glass and carried it to the front porch. She pushed her black curls off her forehead. She watched the cars go by. Little children played in the yard next door.

"Hey, Haley!" someone yelled.

Haley looked up, surprised. There on the sidewalk stood Scott Bailey. He held a big, colorful skateboard under his arm. He wore dark sunglasses, shorts, and a T-shirt.

"You look like someone just ran over your dog," said Scott.

"I don't have a dog," said Haley.

"Well, maybe *that's* your problem," said Scott. "Every kid should have a dog. I've got *two* of them."

Haley sipped from her lemonade. *Maybe if I just ignore him, he'll go away,* she thought. *Boys are so gross! And Scott Bailey is the grossest.* Scott walked closer and held his arm out for Haley to see. "Look!" he said. "I did that skateboarding."

Haley saw a big, dark scab on Scott's elbow. A crooked red scratch traced down from the scab. Roughened skin surrounded the scratch.

"Yuck!" said Haley. "You must be a pretty bad skateboarder. What'd you do? Trip over an ant?"

Scott inspected his arm. "I got this going down Dead Man's Curve," he said proudly. "You know, the hill behind the school."

"You call that a hill?" asked Haley.

Scott pressed his lips together. Then pointing at Haley, he said, "Well, what happened to your hair? Did you get caught in an egg beater?"

"Get lost!" said Haley. She patted her hair,

68

and it felt the same way it always did—soft and curly. He was trying to be mean.

Scott grinned. He placed one foot on his skateboard. With his other foot, he pushed himself along the sidewalk. Soon he was out of sight, and Haley breathed a sigh of relief.

He thinks he's so cool just because he'll be in seventh grade, she thought. *And there's nothing wrong with my hair! It's just like Lauren's—only shorter.*

Haley looked up at the sound of a car engine. Gary pulled his car up to the curb and parked in front of the Boster house. Lauren hopped out of the car. She waved good-bye as Gary drove away. Then she walked to the porch.

"Hi," said Haley. "Are you still mad at me?"

Lauren pursed her lips together. Then she smiled. "I guess not," she said reaching out to pat Haley's shoulder. "It's just that my diary is very private."

"I'm sorry," said Haley. "I won't ever do it

again." She brightened now that it was clear that Lauren wasn't angry with her.

"Do you want to shoot some hoops?" asked Haley. "I put air in the basketball today."

"No thanks, Haley," said Lauren. "I've got to take a shower and get ready. Gary and I are going out for hamburgers tonight." Opening the door, she disappeared into the house.

"Gee," Haley whispered to herself. "It's like I don't even have a sister anymore."

* * * * *

That night, Haley lay in bed listening to the night sounds outside her bedroom window. She heard an owl, crickets, music, and laughter from a neighbor's house. She was almost asleep when she heard Gary's car pull up in front of the house. A moment later, the front door opened, and footsteps came up the stairs. Lauren closed the bathroom door. Then Haley heard it open again, and Lauren's bedroom door being closed.

Haley climbed out of bed. Walking quietly down the hall, she tapped lightly on Lauren's bedroom door.

"Come in," said Lauren.

Haley opened the door. She saw Lauren sitting at the dresser holding her diary. She held a pen in her other hand. Lauren closed the diary and returned it to its drawer.

Haley closed the door behind her. She climbed onto Lauren's bed and sat cross-legged. She watched while Lauren wiped her eye makeup off with tissues.

"What did you do today?" asked Lauren.

"Not much," said Haley. "I cleaned out my tent. And I talked to this really gross boy. And I helped Mom weed the tomato garden."

Haley leaned back against Lauren's pillow. She sighed contentedly. After all, this was the way things used to be. Here they were, together in their nightgowns, sharing a late night talk.

"This is nice, isn't it?" asked Haley, gazing

at Lauren. "I mean, it's nice for us to be together just the two of us. Isn't it?"

Lauren smiled at Haley, knowing what she was referring to. "Yes," she said. "This is nice. I am glad we're sisters, you know?"

"You are?" asked Haley, surprised.

"Of course, Haley," said Lauren. She ran a brush through her long, dark hair. "You're a great little sister, even if you are a pain sometimes."

Haley knew that Lauren was talking about the diary. She grinned sheepishly. "You're a great big sister, too" she said eagerly, hoping that Lauren would remember this moment.

Lauren stood up from the dresser. She walked over to the bed and sat down on the edge. Haley looked into her sister's face and thought about how pretty she was.

Haley felt happy and sad at the same time. She felt happy to be sharing some private time with her sister. But she also knew that Gary was still in Lauren's thoughts, and that

Lauren cared about him, too. Haley felt these private times were becoming rare. Maybe they wouldn't be together tomorrow or the next day. Things were changing, and Haley wanted to stop the changes from happening.

Haley breathed in deeply. "Are you tired of Gary yet?" she asked, hesitantly.

Lauren looked surprised. Then a smile tugged at the corners of her mouth. "No," she said, staring dreamily up at the ceiling. "He's always fun to be with. He's the most amazing guy I've ever met! Did you know he even knows how to play the guitar?"

Haley shook her head. "Is he taking beginner lessons?" she asked.

"No," said Lauren. "He's really good. He's played for a long time."

"Oh. Don't you think he's kind of funny looking?" asked Haley hopefully.

Lauren shook her head. Soft curls brushed across her shoulders.

"No," she said. "I think he's really cute. And

73

he's really sensitive, too," said Lauren, with a sigh.

Haley decided to change the subject. "I'm going to summer camp in one week," she announced. "They have softball teams there. Last year I played outfield. I hope I get to pitch this year. I think I'd be a pretty good pitcher if someone would just give me a chance."

Lauren cocked her head to one side, still deep in thought. "To me, Gary's a really special kind of guy," she said.

Haley frowned. "Dad says he'll help me learn how to pitch," she said. "But he just hasn't had time lately."

"I love the smell of his after-shave," said Lauren.

"Dad's?" asked Haley, surprised.

"No, silly," giggled Lauren. "Gary's."

Haley studied her sister closely. She thought, *It's as if my sister has a disease. It's Mush Disease, and all its victims can think about is romance and mush like that.*

"Oh, Gary," sighed Lauren. She hugged a pillow to her chest and flopped back onto the bed.

This is the worst case of Mush Disease I've ever seen, thought Haley. *But if anyone can cure Mush Disease, it's me! And I'd better do something fast!*

Five

WITH just a week left before summer camp, Haley and Anna walked to the Parkland public pool. Shrieking kids were everywhere, which Haley thought added to the excitement. On the grass around the swimming pool, mothers and children stretched out on colorful beach towels.

Haley and Anna changed into their swim suits in the dressing room.

"That's the same suit you had last year, isn't it?" asked Anna.

"Yeah," admitted Haley. "Mom said I could either have a new swim suit or a new tennis racket. I picked the racket."

The girls walked out into the bright, hot

sunshine and spread their towels over a patch of grass beside an unoccupied red beach towel. Looking around, Haley noticed Scott Bailey standing beside the pool.

"Oh, gross!" she said. "Look who's here."

Haley watched as Scott grabbed Amy Edwards, a cute blond going into seventh grade, around the waist to throw her into the pool. Amy shrieked and tossed her hair around.

"If I were her, I'd put an elbow into his stomach," said Haley.

"But look. She *likes* it," said Anna. "Look at her! She's really laughing."

"Yeah, but she's in *seventh* grade," explained Haley.

"I hope *we* don't get like that when *we're* in seventh grade," said Anna.

"Don't worry about it," Haley said. "We won't. We've even taken a pledge." Haley spread tanning oil up and down her arms. Then she put white ointment on her nose to keep it from burning.

Amy Edwards dropped down onto the red towel next to Haley. Haley watched as Amy stretched out on her stomach. Amy waved at someone in the pool. "Scott Bailey!" she yelled, giggling. "You just quit teasing me, you big, old meanie!"

"Big old *weirdo* is more like it," whispered Haley, rolling her eyes at Anna.

Suddenly, a wave of cold water splashed onto Haley's back. Part of it hit Amy Edwards. Amy squealed. Haley jumped up in time to see Scott standing in the pool. He held onto the edge, laughing.

Haley turned to Amy. "If he splashes me again, he's going to be dead meat. Have you ever met a grosser guy?"

Amy batted her eyelashes. "I think he's kind of cute," she said. "Actually, I like him."

"You can't be serious?" asked Haley, in disbelief. She wrung out the corner of her towel that had become wet from Scott's

splashing and then spread it out again.

"Sure, I'm serious," said Amy. "But then, you're only in sixth grade, right? That explains it."

Anna moved onto Haley's towel. The two friends sat side by side listening to the more experienced seventh grader.

"You both will like boys, too, eventually," Amy insisted.

"No way!" exclaimed Haley.

"Forget it," Anna joined in.

Amy smiled knowingly. Then she glanced back over toward the pool at Scott, and waved at him.

"We've taken an oath," Haley explained. "It's part of a secret club that we have. It's called The Boy Busters Club, and our tent is headquarters. Do you want to be a member with us?"

Amy looked curious. "What kind of club is it?" she asked.

"Boy Buster members promise to never like

boys and to never do wimpy girl stuff," Haley explained seriously.

Amy pulled a bottle of cologne from her purse. Dabbing it on her wrists, she asked, "What kind of wimpy girl stuff?"

"We won't wear makeup," said Anna.

"And we won't wear high heels or electric rollers either. And we won't go to dances or on dates," added Haley.

"And we'll never wear lace," said Anna.

"Boy Busters don't kiss," continued Haley, wrinkling her nose. "Unless it's your dog or cat or parents, of course."

"You can't kiss boys?" Amy asked in amusement.

"No way. Do you want to join?" Haley waited eagerly for Amy's answer.

Amy opened her purse and pulled a book out. Haley quickly read the title: *Love in the Shadows*. The cover picture showed a tan man with his muscular arms wrapped around a beautiful, blond woman.

"I really do like boys," Amy admitted apologetically. "You will, too, one of these days. *All* girls start liking boys."

"Count me out," said Haley. "I'm allergic to all that mush stuff."

Amy opened her book and began to read. Anna returned to her towel. She sat down as Haley turned toward her.

Haley's voice sunk to a whisper. "What if she's right?" she asked. "Do you think she's right, that we're going to get Mush Disease someday, too?"

Anna shrugged her shoulders. "Maybe it's not so bad," she said hesitantly. "Maybe boys get better when they get older."

"Anna, are you serious?" exclaimed Haley. "Have you forgotten our pledge? We're *never* going to like boys. Boys are the worst. They tease girls. They cut in front of girls in the lunch line at school. They make fun of girls' hair if it's curly. They try to knock girls down with the ball whenever they play kick ball. And when boys get older, they try to kiss you. Yuck!"

"No one's ever tried to kiss *me*," said Anna.

"That's because you don't have Mush Disease," explained Haley.

Anna nodded slowly. "I guess you're right," she said.

Haley looked around at the kids. Older boys and girls tossed a beach ball in the pool. They dunked each other and shrieked and giggled.

"When did Lauren catch Mush Disease?" asked Anna.

"I think she must've caught it from Gary," said Haley. "She dated other guys before Gary, but she didn't go nuts over them like she has with Gary."

"How old was she when she first began to like boys?" asked Anna.

Haley rubbed her chin. "I don't know," she said. "And Lauren's never home much these days for me to ask her about it."

Suddenly, Amy Edwards jumped up from her towel, shrieking. Some ice cubes rolled off her back. "Scott Bailey!" she squealed. "I'm going to get you for this!" Amy ran close behind Scott and jumped into the pool after him. She grabbed at his arms and tried to dunk him under the water.

"It's Mush Disease all right," Anna said.

Haley nodded. Her eyebrows came together in the middle. "I'm worried," she said. "I don't ever want to act like a jerk about boys."

"At least if it's going to happen, I'd like to know *when* it's going to happen so I can be prepared for it," said Anna with a heavy sigh. She picked at a scab on her arm.

Haley breathed in deeply. She narrowed her eyes. "I know how we can find out when Lauren got the disease," she whispered.

"How?" asked Anna eagerly. Her eyes widened with curiosity.

There was a moment of silence. Then Haley whispered, "Lauren's diary. We can flip through it and find out when Lauren first started feeling mushy about boys."

Anna clenched her teeth together. "I don't know," she said hesitantly. "You know what your mother and Lauren said about snooping. You'll be in *big* trouble this time if we get caught."

"Don't worry," said Haley confidently. "Nobody ever gets caught twice."

Six

THE sun was setting as Haley and Anna faced each other in the Boy Busters Headquarters. Haley poked her head out of the tent and stared up at Lauren's window through the oversized binoculars.

"She's still here," Haley warned. "But Gary's picking her up any minute now."

Anna chewed her bottom lip in anticipation. "You know," she said. "I'm sort of afraid to read Lauren's diary."

"Why?" asked Haley. "I told you no one gets caught twice."

"Well, it's not that," said Anna slowly. "What if we find out that we'll start liking boys in sixth grade? That means we only have two and a half more months to be normal. What'll we do?"

"Don't worry," said Haley. "I don't think Mush Disease strikes until *after* the sixth grade."

"I don't know." Anna shook her head doubtfully.

"Listen!" Haley turned an ear toward the house. "It's Gary's car," she said. The girls waited quietly for a few minutes, and then the car's engine whirred to life again. It faded slowly as they drove off down the road together.

"She's gone," said Haley. "Let's get going!"

Haley ran through the yard with Anna close behind her. The kitchen was empty. Haley sighed with relief. "The coast is clear," she whispered.

Creeping through the dining room, Haley was careful to not make a sound. Then, climbing the stairs, she heard her mother call, "Haley! Is that you?"

Haley gritted her teeth together. "Uh, yeah,

Mom," she answered back.

"Haley, come here, please," Mrs. Boster called.

Haley and Anna looked at each other with worried expressions. They followed the sound of Mrs. Boster's voice into the laundry room. Mrs. Boster stood beside the ironing board. A stack of shorts and T-shirts lay neatly folded at the end of the table. Haley loved the clean smell of warm, freshly ironed clothes.

Mrs. Boster glanced up as Haley and Anna came into the room. She held up a T-shirt for Haley to see. Pointing at the neck, she said, "I'm putting name tags on all your summer camp clothes, so you won't lose anything, okay?"

"Okay, Mom," Haley said. The name tags made her feel like a little kid, but she wasn't about to argue now.

Mrs. Boster turned her gaze to Anna. "Did you ask your mom if it's okay to stay here again tonight?" she asked.

"Yes. She said it's okay," said Anna, nodding.

Haley's mother spread some wrinkled jeans out on the ironing board. "I don't know how you girls can spend so much time in that tent," she said. "Aren't you tired of it?"

"No," said Haley. "We're becoming experts at camping."

Haley and Anna left the room. Without a word, Haley motioned to Anna to follow her. They tiptoed up the stairs and down the hall. Haley gently placed her hand over the knob to Lauren's bedroom, and slowly turned it. She carefully pushed the door open, feeling her heart pound in her chest as she entered her sister's room.

Anna tiptoed behind her across the room. Haley opened Lauren's dresser drawer. She reached in under the silk scarves. Her fingers searched every inch of the drawer, but the diary wasn't there.

Haley turned to Anna and silently shrugged

as if to say, "Now what do we do?"

Anna shrugged back.

Haley opened another drawer in the dresser. It was full of boxes and tubes of cosmetics, but there was no diary. Haley frowned and walked over to Lauren's bed. She slid her hand under the pillow. Nothing was there either.

Haley knelt beside the bed and looked underneath it. There was nothing there. And then she slid her hand between the mattress and box springs and wiggled her fingers around.

Suddenly, her eyes grew wide with excitement. She smiled, and Anna knew they'd found it. *Inside were the answers*, Anna thought, with a sick feeling in her stomach.

Haley pulled the pink and blue diary from its hiding place, and held it triumphantly up in the air for Anna to see. Then the two girls sat cross-legged on the floor. Haley hurriedly opened the diary. There was that same neat,

little writing that she'd seen before.

A sudden sound made the girls look up. Noisy footsteps came clattering down the hall. Haley looked frantically for a place to throw the diary, but then relaxed when the footsteps continued on down the stairs. She turned her eyes back to the diary.

Pointing at an entry, Haley whispered, "Read this!"

Anna leaned closer and read:

April 17—Today was a good day at school. Jim Roberts sat with me at lunch. He's so cute! Marcia says he's not dating anyone. I hope he asks me out!

Haley wrinkled her nose. "Mush, mush, and more mush," she whispered.

Anna nodded. In a hushed voice, she said, "Look in the earlier pages. We've got to find out exactly *when* Lauren got Mush Disease."

Haley turned back to March. Flipping

through the pages, she stopped and pointed at another entry. She and Anna read:

March 17—Today I took Haley to the movies. We had a nice time. I let Haley have two ice cream sandwiches after the movie.

Haley turned dreamy eyed at the memory. She licked her lips. "Ah, the good old days," she said. Haley turned back to February. She stopped at an entry that read:

February 8—Stan Deason called me to-night. Boy, was I surprised! He asked me about a homework assignment. But he acted really nervous. I think he wanted to ask me out, but he was too afraid. He really has a nice voice.

Haley flipped back through January, stopping to read several of the entries. "Hmm," she said. "I think that Mush Disease kind of creeps up on you. Lauren liked boys okay for awhile. But then, she suddenly went nuts when she met Gary. She was *kind of* mushy before him, but with him she became *completely* mushy."

Anna looked around nervously. "Come on. Let's get out of here before we get caught," she said.

Haley stuffed the diary back under the mattress. And then she put her ear against Lauren's door. No sound came from the other side. She carefully opened the door and looked up and down the hallway. Nodding to Anna, she gave the signal that the coast was clear.

The two girls crept down the stairs. As they entered the kitchen, they stopped abruptly at the sight of Mr. Boster. He was closing the refrigerator door.

"Oh!" exclaimed Haley's father. "I didn't know you girls were in the house. My, you've been quiet."

Haley smiled uneasily. "We were just—uh—

just—" She couldn't think of an answer.

"Reading," Anna said, coming to the rescue.

Haley and Anna left the kitchen and returned to their backyard tent. Haley wiped her hand across her forehead. "Boy, that was close," she said.

Crawling into the tent, Haley and Anna stretched out on top of their sleeping bags. Haley lay staring up at the ceiling.

"I guess you start liking boys a little," Haley said, "and then one day you meet someone who makes you crazy."

"Not me," said Anna, determinedly.

"Me either," said Haley. "I hereby pledge again *never* to like boys—especially Gary."

Haley turned onto her stomach and reached for the bag of potato chips. "Of course, there will be boys at summer camp, too," Haley said.

"Yeah," said Anna sadly. "But at least they're on the other side of the lake."

Haley swatted at a mosquito on her arm. "I can't wait to learn how to pitch a softball," she said.

"Are you going to try out for captain of the team?" asked Anna.

"Sure," said Haley confidently.

The girls lay quietly for a while listening to the night sounds outside the tent. As it grew darker, Haley turned on her flashlight. "Look at this," she said. Holding the flashlight under her chin, she opened her mouth and bugged her eyes. "Ooo gross!" squealed Anna. "You look like a vampire."

Next, Haley stretched her mouth as wide as she could. She covered the bright end of the flashlight with her lips.

Anna laughed. "You look like a Halloween pumpkin," she said.

Haley laughed and took the flashlight out of her mouth. She said, "Did you ever hear the story about the campers who got trapped up in the mountains? There was an escaped convict with a hook for a hand. He caught one of the campers. Then do you know what happened?" she asked ominously.

Anna gulped. With a nervous laugh, she asked, "Did he pierce her ears for her?"

"No-o-o," said Haley in a deep, growly voice. "He took his hook and he..."

Haley stopped talking. She put her ear to the tent wall, listening carefully. "Did you hear that?" she asked.

"Wh-what?" asked Anna. She scrunched her knees up against her chest and wrapped her arms around them.

In a hushed voice, Haley said, "It sounds like a hook cutting into the tent."

The sound of scraping came from the tent wall near Haley. Anna screamed. Haley laughed.

"*You* were making that sound!" exclaimed Anna. "You jerk! You almost gave me a heart attack."

"Beware of the hook," said Haley, laughing

again. She scraped a fingernail along the canvas wall.

Haley grew suddenly quiet. "Did you hear that?" she asked.

Anna leaned back onto her sleeping bag. "Give me a break," she said. "I'm not going to fall for that trick again."

Haley shook her head. "No," she said. "I really mean it this time. Listen!"

Haley listened to the sound of a car pulling up in front of her house. "It's Gary and Lauren," she whispered.

"Should we go spy on them?" asked Anna.

"Nah." Haley stretched back onto her sleeping bag. "We've seen them before."

"I bet they're walking up to the front porch," Anna whispered.

"I bet they're holding hands," said Haley in a pained voice.

"What are they doing now?" asked Anna.

Haley pulled a pillow on top of her head. "I don't even want to think about it," she said.

"It's mushy, gooey, gross stuff."

"Kissing?" asked Anna.

Haley moaned in answer. She pulled the pillow away from her head and sat up. "We better take the pledge again," she said.

"Okay." Anna placed her hand over her heart. Haley did the same.

"We promise that we will never like boys, or dates, or makeup," said Haley.

"And we'll never do wimpy girl stuff," added Anna.

"And we'll never shave our legs and talk on the phone all day like Lauren does," vowed Haley.

The two friends clasped hands together. Then they spit out of the tent door to make the pledge official.

"Oh! There's one more thing!" Haley cried. She placed her hand over her heart again. "I promise that I'll get my sister back from Gary if it's the last thing I do."

"And how are you going to do that, Haley?"

asked Anna doubtfully.

Haley shrugged her shoulders in the dark. "I don't know yet," she said. "But I'll think of a way."

Seven

"MOM! Dad!" yelled Lauren urgently. Haley watched as her older sister came running down the stairs. Lauren held a small pink and blue book in her hand. Haley gulped when she saw it was the diary.

Lauren's voice was angry. "She's done it again!" she shouted. Turning to Haley, she said, "You promised to quit snooping! Why did you do it?"

Haley stood speechless. Her parents turned their serious eyes toward her. Lauren waved the diary under Haley's nose.

"I know you read it," Lauren accused. "It wasn't in the same place where I left it. And you bent some of the pages up."

Haley felt her knees tremble. She thought, *What can I say? I can't lie. Maybe I could run away. But I don't have anywhere to go. Oh, why does Lauren hate me so much?*

Mr. Boster said in a deep voice, "Is that true, Haley? Did you read your sister's diary again?"

There was no escape. Haley confessed. Softly, she said, "Yes."

There was a moment of quiet while Haley felt the disappointment all around her.

"Why can't I have any privacy?" wailed Lauren. "Do I have to put a lock and chain on my bedroom door to keep you from snooping?"

"I'm sorry," said Haley.

"That's what you said *last* time," huffed Lauren. She glared down at Haley. "I just can't understand why you do this."

Mrs. Boster said, "Haley, you have to respect Lauren's privacy. You can't snoop through her diary whenever you feel like it."

I don't do it whenever I feel like it, Haley

thought. *I've only done it twice.*

Mrs. Boster looked serious. She said, "If you get into your sister's diary again, you will be punished."

"Punished?" Haley's chin began to tremble.

"Yes," said Mrs. Boster. "You will be punished. There will be no summer camp."

Lauren held the diary tightly in her hand. Her voice rose with anger. "But camp is *tomorrow*," she said. "Big deal. But what about when she gets back from camp?"

Mr. Boster's voice sounded stern. He said, "If you're caught snooping again, Haley, you won't get that pro softball and glove you've been wanting for your birthday."

Haley hung her head. She felt scared and embarrassed at the same time. She was afraid that she'd never get the softball she wanted so badly. And she was embarrassed that, once again, here she was at the center of all the attention. Only this wasn't the kind of attention she had had in mind.

Boy, Haley thought, *it seems like everyone's always yelling at me.*

Lauren stomped up the stairs, the diary tucked underneath her arm. Mr. Boster returned to his newspaper, and Mrs. Boster returned to the kitchen to finish filling her cosmetics orders.

Haley walked out of the house and breathed in the fresh air. She got her basketball from the garage and began shooting hoops in the driveway. *Maybe I'll just play basketball and sleep in a tent for the rest of my life,* she thought. *That way I won't get in anyone's way.*

Haley turned at the sound of a car engine. She frowned as Gary parked his car. He waved at Haley, then walked up to the front door. Haley dribbled the ball, dodging imaginary opponents. Then she aimed the ball for the basketball hoop. It rolled around the rim, then fell through the basket.

"Mind if I shoot a few?"

Haley jumped at the sound of a man's voice.

She turned around to find Gary standing behind her.

"Lauren's not ready yet," he explained. "I thought I'd come out here and shoot a few baskets with you."

Haley held onto the basketball. Then, reluctantly, she threw the ball to Gary. He dribbled, spun around, then leaped into the air to slam dunk the ball. It went through the net and bounced onto the driveway.

Haley caught the ball and shot. It hit the backboard and rolled off the side.

"Try arcing the ball when you shoot it," Gary advised. "It should drop down through the center of the basket. You can work on the bank shots later."

Haley stared at Gary. She tried to see what it was that Lauren liked so much. But she just couldn't figure it out. *After all, his ears looked too big,* Haley thought. *And he wasn't good enough for Lauren. That was the truth,* Haley told herself.

Gary passed the basketball to Haley. She dribbled the ball as Gary guarded her. She threw the ball wildly into the air.

"Don't freak out when someone's guarding you," said Gary with a smile. "Just try to dribble around me. Fake me out."

He's going to think I can't talk, Haley thought. *But I just can't think of anything to say. What can you say to a guy who's stealing your sister away from you? If it wasn't for him, Lauren wouldn't be mad at me.*

"Hi, Gary," Lauren said, walking across the driveway. Haley noticed the fresh lipstick and eye shadow. Lauren was wearing her favorite blue dress, which meant she and Gary were going somewhere special.

"See you later, Haley," Gary said in a friendly voice. He passed the ball back to Haley.

Haley said, "Good-bye." She could tell from Lauren's face that she was still mad about the diary.

Lauren hooked her arm through Gary's

arm. Together they walked to Gary's car and drove off. Suddenly, Haley didn't feel like shooting baskets anymore. She took the ball and slammed it down onto the driveway. It bounced above her head and rolled onto the lawn.

"Ooo! Somebody's got a temper!"

Haley whirled around at the sound of his voice. "Scott," she said with a frown. "What are you doing here?"

"I was just riding by," Scott said, climbing down from his bicycle. He walked it up the driveway toward Haley.

"What's the problem?" he asked. "Every time I see you, you look like you're mad about something."

Normally, Haley wouldn't have said anything at all to Scott. But she was still upset. After all, her parents and her sister were mad at her. And a stupid old boy named Gary was ruining her life.

"It's my sister," Haley admitted. "She's

dating this guy. And they're together *all* the time."

"Yeah," said Scott. "I saw them drive down the street. He looked like an okay guy."

Haley shot Scott an angry glance. "She never spends time with *me* anymore," she muttered.

"Maybe it's your breath," suggested Scott.

Haley noticed that he was grinning. But she didn't find anything funny about the situation. She suddenly realized that talking with Scott was getting her nowhere. After all, he was a boy, wasn't he? She reminded herself that all boys are nothing but trouble.

"Go away," said Haley. "You're getting on my nerves."

Scott grinned from ear to ear. "Maybe *you're* the one who gets on your *sister's* nerves," he suggested. "Maybe she thinks you're a super pain. I'll bet that's why she hangs out with him. She's probably afraid she'll be stuck with *you*. If you ask me, she's avoiding you because you're so weird and so mean."

Haley grabbed the basketball from the ground. "I'm going to bounce this off your head if you don't get out of my yard!" she threatened.

"See what I mean," said Scott. "I feel sorry for the guy who ever has *you* for a girlfriend."

"I'll *never* have a boyfriend!" shouted Haley.

"I believe you," said Scott. He turned his bike around and hopped up onto the seat. Pedaling down the drive, he called over his shoulder, "A guy would have to be crazy to like a girl like you."

Haley shook her fist at Scott as he disappeared down the sidewalk. Then she walked into the backyard to Boy Busters Headquarters. She crawled into the tent and plopped onto the ground.

Suddenly, Haley felt worried. *What if Scott's right?* she asked herself. *Maybe Lauren hates me. Maybe she's with Gary all*

the time because she doesn't want to be with me! Maybe she doesn't like me anymore. If she did like me, she wouldn't ignore me all the time, would she? She hardly ever talks to me anymore.

A big tear formed in Haley's eye. It slid down her nose and plopped onto the canvas floor.

When did she quit liking me? Haley wondered. *What did I do to make her stop liking me?*

Haley knew where the answer to that question could be found—in Lauren's diary. *But I promised I wouldn't snoop anymore.* Haley reminded herself. *But this would be the very last time,* she promised herself. *And it's the only way I can find out whether or not Lauren still likes me. She writes everything in her diary.*

"I'll be extra careful this time," Haley whispered to herself. "I'll put it back in the exact place. And I won't bend any of the pages."

Haley felt her heart beating wildly. The coast was clear downstairs. Haley made sure that both her mom and her dad were watching TV in the family room. Then, quietly, she walked upstairs. Looking quickly around, she opened the door to Lauren's room and walked in. Slowly, Haley closed the door behind her.

She crept across the blue carpet to the dresser drawer. Just as she suspected, the diary was not hidden beneath the silk scarves. It wasn't under the mattress either.

Haley opened Lauren's closet. She looked at all the brightly colored clothes hanging there. There were skirts, dresses, slacks, and blouses. There didn't appear to be a diary hidden on the shelf. Kneeling down, Haley reached for a shoe box. She opened the lid. Inside she found a pair of shoes. Haley lifted the top from another shoe box. Sure enough, there was the diary peeping out from beneath the tissue paper.

Haley felt excited and scared as she lifted

the diary from the box. Quickly, she flipped through the pages. She finally reached the last entry, opened the book wide, and gasped as she saw what was written there.

Eight

HALEY'S hand began to tremble as she read the diary entry again.

June 21—I have wonderful news! Gary and I are running away together tomorrow. Gary and I will drive to Missouri. It's so exciting, because nobody knows! I'm meeting him at the water tower at 9:00 tomorrow morning. Just imagine, tomorrow, Gary and I will be married!

Haley closed the diary and dropped the book back into the shoe box.

This is the absolute worst, she thought. *Lauren's going for the biggest mush of all—marriage!*

Haley looked around the blue bedroom. She was scared that she would never see her sister again. She called Anna on the telephone, but no one was home. Haley hung up the phone and whispered to herself, "Oh, Anna, where are you when I need you? We need to have an emergency Boy Busters meeting! I need your help."

Haley spent a sleepless night in bed. Over and over in her mind, she wondered about what she should do. *Should I tell Mom and Dad?* she asked herself. *No, they'll get upset, and Lauren will get in trouble. Then she'll hate me even more. And they'll want to know how I found out. If I tell them I read her diary, then I won't be able to go to camp tomorrow.*

Haley tossed and turned in her bed. She was almost asleep when she heard Lauren come home. Sounds came from Lauren's room, and Haley wondered if her sister might be packing.

Should I go talk to her? wondered Haley.

*But then if I do, I'll be in trouble. And I won't
be able to go to camp.*

It was a big problem. Haley thought and
thought about it until she finally fell asleep.
She dreamed that she was at summer camp.
There were volleyball games, archery, running,
swimming, fishing, and softball going on.

In the dream, she stood on the pitcher's
mound winding up for a pitch. Anna squat-
ted behind home plate with a catcher's mask
covering her face. Scott Bailey walked up to
home plate and raised his bat. Haley pitched
the ball as hard as she could. Scott swung.
Crack came the sound of the bat hitting the
ball. The ball flew straight toward Haley, fast
as a bullet. She reached her hand out to catch
it. But when she saw that she wasn't wearing
a glove, she pulled her hand back. The ball
sailed past her as Scott ran for first base.

"Why didn't you catch it, Haley?" a team-
mate called.

"Yeah, Boster, why didn't you catch it?"

someone shouted angrily.

Haley woke up, her face covered in sweat. The sun was shining through the window. Outside it was a perfect Sunday morning. But inside, Haley didn't feel very perfect. In fact, she felt very confused.

Haley jumped out of bed and pulled on shorts and a T-shirt. A knock loomed at the door. Mrs. Boster called, "Haley, get up! We leave for the bus in one hour!"

But Haley knew what she had to do—even if it meant giving up her camping trip. She decided to talk to Lauren, and ask her not to run away with Gary. Maybe she'd get herself into trouble and have to stay home. *But,* Haley told herself, *I'd rather have my older sister than two weeks at camp. And Lauren's even better than a new softball and glove.*

Haley threw open her bedroom door. She raced down the hall and banged on Lauren's door. There was no answer.

"What's all the noise?" asked Mr. Boster,

sticking his head out of his bedroom.

"Where's Lauren?" asked Haley breathlessly.

"I don't know," said Mr. Boster. "Maybe your mother knows."

Haley ran downstairs. She found her mother in the kitchen reading the newspaper.

"What's the rush?" asked Mrs. Boster. "Don't worry. We'll get you to the bus in plenty of time."

"Where's Lauren?" asked Haley, looking around wildly.

Mrs. Boster wiped her hands on her apron. "She left early with Gary," she said. "I think they were going to visit some friends of Gary's."

"Is that what she told you?" asked Haley. Her fingers played nervously with her curly hair.

"Haley, what's wrong?" asked Mrs. Boster. She looked concerned. "Did you want to say good-bye to Lauren?" she asked sympathetically. "I'm sorry, Haley. But you know how Lauren has been lately. I'm afraid she must've forgotten that you leave for camp today. I'm sure she'll be sorry that she didn't get to say good-bye to you."

Haley turned and ran from the kitchen. Stopping for a moment to think, she suddenly knew what the answer was. "I'll go catch Lauren at the water tower," Haley whispered to herself. "That's where she's meeting Gary. If I can get there in time, I can stop them from running away."

Without a second to spare, Haley ran from the house. She broke into a brisk trot. She ran on the sidewalk, passing house after house. Her breath became ragged. But still, she kept on running. She kept her eyes on the distant water tower that stretched high into the air.

Haley chanted a rhythm to herself as she ran. *Lauren, please don't go, please don't go,* she pleaded to herself. If she could say it all the way to the tower, Haley thought maybe it would come true.

Little children stopped to stare at Haley as she ran along. She huffed and puffed, but still she kept running. At last she drew near the water tower. A cement sidewalk led up to the giant steel structure.

Haley trotted up the sidewalk. She walked around the tower. No one was there. *Was she too late? Had they already left?*

Haley ran around the tower one more time to make sure that no one was hiding from her. *"Lauren, please don't go!"* she whispered under her breath.

Flopping down onto the ground, Haley leaned back against the tower. Her chest heaved as she breathed heavily. Her head spun with thoughts of Lauren. *Is she married already? Are she and Gary driving to Missouri? Is all this my fault?*

Haley thought back to all the good times she and Lauren had shared. She thought about the time Lauren took her to the zoo, and about the time Lauren bought her a basketball for her birthday. Haley remembered all the fun, secrets, and memories they had shared together over the years. They used to make tents in the house with blankets, sheets, and chairs.

They crawled around under the blankets, pretending they really were camping.

Hot tears filled Haley's eyes. "It's all my fault," she moaned out loud. "I should never have snooped in Lauren's diary and made her mad at me."

Haley rubbed the tears out of her eyes. She wiped her nose on her T-shirt. "It's Gary's fault, too," she said angrily. "Everything was okay until he came along. Lauren liked me until he messed everything up. *Boys ruin everything.*

More tears filled her eyes. Haley cried when she thought about never seeing her sister again. "Oh, Lauren!" she sobbed.

A look at her watch showed Haley that it was 9:15. "Uh- oh," she said. "I'm in big trouble now. Mom and Dad will wonder where I am. The camp bus left 15 minutes ago."

Haley heaved a big sigh. "Oh well," she said. "I hope Anna has fun, and I hope *she's* not mad at me, too, for missing the bus."

Maybe I should run away, Haley thought desperately. *After all, Mom and Dad will be furious. I'll probably get punished for the rest of my life. And I don't have an older sister, anymore.*

Haley looked up at the clouds overhead. "I wish I could jump up onto a cloud and float away," she said.

"Where would you go?" asked a familiar voice behind her.

Haley jumped up at the sound of the voice. "Lauren!" she shouted.

Lauren and Gary stood together, looking down at Haley.

Haley's voice broke as she looked into her

sister's big blue eyes. "Please don't leave, Lauren," she begged. "I promise I'll never snoop again. I promise. Please don't go away."

Lauren put her hands on her hips, while Gary shoved his hands into his pockets.

"What makes you think I'm going away?" asked Lauren.

Haley was stunned. "I-it said...I read it...I mean...uh...it was in your..."

"In my diary?" asked Lauren, softly.

Haley felt the blood rush into her face. Silently, she nodded.

Gary said gently, "Haley, we're not getting married. At least not right now." He looked tenderly at Lauren, who smiled back at him.

Haley felt puzzled. She chewed her bottom lip. "But it said in your diary that you were going to Missouri," she insisted.

Haley saw the grin on her sister's face. Suddenly, she knew.

"It was a trick!" she exclaimed. "You played a rotten trick on me."

Lauren nodded. "I just wanted to see if you'd keep out of my diary," she said. "I wanted to find out if you would keep your promise."

Haley saw the disappointment on her sister's face. Tears rushed to her eyes and trickled down her cheeks. "I had to read it," she said, as big tears rolled down her cheeks. "You don't love me anymore, and I had to know why."

Lauren looked shocked. She slid an arm around Haley's shaking shoulders. To Gary, she said, "Please wait in the car. I think Haley and I need to talk a little, sister to sister."

Gary nodded and walked away.

Lauren sat down on the ground, pulling Haley down with her. Haley stopped crying. She saw with relief that her sister didn't look angry anymore.

"What's on your mind?" asked Lauren.

Haley spilled her heart out. All the weeks of worry and doubt came rushing out in a flood of words.

"You're with Gary all the time," said Haley.

"You never want to be with *me*. Do you hate me?"

Lauren listened quietly. Then she leaned over and kissed the top of Haley's head. "I'm sorry," Lauren said. "I didn't know you were feeling so low. I guess I've been so caught up with Gary that I haven't noticed much of anything lately."

Lauren sighed. She took Haley's hand and looked deeply into her eyes. "I love you," she said. "I always have. I always will. You're my sister. And that's very special. But," she added, "that doesn't mean that I won't care for anyone else."

"Do you mean Gary?" asked Haley, looking sad again.

Lauren nodded her head. "Gary is my friend. I like him a lot. I can care for you and Gary at the same time."

Haley bit her lip to keep from crying again. "But I never get to see you, anymore," she said sadly.

Lauren looked apologetic. "I'm sorry," she said. "You're right. I should spend more time with you. In fact, I'd like it if you would come with Gary and me sometimes. There are lots of things that we all would enjoy doing together."

"What?" exclaimed Haley. "You want me to go on a date with you and Gary?"

"Sure," nodded Lauren. "Gary wouldn't mind. He likes you."

"He does?" asked Haley doubtfully.

"Of course he does," Lauren said. "If you'd give him a chance, he'd be your friend, too."

"But there's one more thing," Lauren added. "You've got to quit snooping through my stuff."

Haley could tell from Lauren's voice that she was serious.

"I've learned my lesson," said Haley sincerely. "Snooping gets me in trouble every time. I won't do it anymore. I'm in enough trouble as it is. Mom and Dad will be super mad when I get home."

"Why? You didn't tell them about this, did you?" asked Lauren curiously.

Haley clenched her teeth together. "No, but I missed the bus to camp. So, they're probably pretty worried by now," she admitted.

"Camp?" exclaimed Lauren. "Oh no! I forgot all about that. Come on. Let's get home quickly."

Lauren jumped to her feet. She smoothed the wrinkles from her slacks. Haley jumped up, too, not noticing the bits of grass stuck to her knees.

Together, they ran down the sidewalk to Gary's car. After all these weeks of listening to its engine roar to and from the house, Haley was finally going to ride in Gary's car. She climbed into the backseat. Lauren scooted onto the front seat beside Gary.

Haley smiled, thinking how she and her sister had worked things out.

She does love me, Haley thought. *She's*

never quit loving me. Everything's going to be okay.

Gary drove through the neighborhood. He turned the corner, and the Boster home came into view. Haley's stomach did a flip-flop as she saw the police car in the driveway. Its red light flashed around and around. Friends and neighbors stood together in groups. There, in the middle of it all, was Scott Bailey with his skateboard under his arm.

Haley saw her parents talking with a police officer. Tears streamed down Mrs. Boster's face as the police officer wrote on a note pad.

"Uh-oh," breathed Haley. "I'm in trouble again."

Nine

GARY pulled his car up in front of the Boster home.

"There she is!" someone shouted.

Haley watched from the car window as people came running. Curious faces peered in at her. *Gee,* she thought, *this must be what it's like to be a rock star.*

Gary and Lauren climbed out of the car. Haley waited in the backseat. A police officer opened the door for her. A silver badge gleamed from his shirt pocket. A gun was strapped to his hip in a black leather holster. He didn't say a word as Haley climbed out of the car.

"Haley!" cried Mrs. Boster. She ran over to the car and hugged Haley. Looking at her closely, she asked, "Are you all right? Where in the world did you go?"

Everyone began crowding around her to hear what she had to say. She blushed with embarrassment. "Sure," she mumbled. "I'm okay."

"We didn't know where you were," said Mr. Boster. "Your mom said you two were talking, and then, suddenly, you were gone. You missed the camp bus, you know."

"I know," said Haley sadly.

The crowd broke up finally, and most people left for home. A few people stood at a distance, watching and waiting for something to happen. Haley caught Scott staring at her. "Gee," he said. "You're kind of young to have the cops after you, aren't you?" He grinned, until he saw the grim look on the police officer's face.

Scott hopped onto his skateboard and rolled quickly away.

Haley inspected the people around her. The

police officer looked stern. Her mother and father seemed to be both relieved and angry. Lauren looked worried. And Gary seemed nervous.

Haley felt like crawling into a hole when she saw the expression on her father's face. "You've got some explaining to do, young lady," he said in a deep voice. "Your mother and I have been worried sick about you."

The police officer kept writing on his note pad, and Haley wondered what he was writing.

"Well, we want some answers. Where were you?" asked Mr. Boster.

Haley shifted uneasily on her feet. "I was at the water tower," she explained in a shaky voice.

"We were together," Lauren hurried to say.

The policeman closed the notebook and slid it into his back pocket. "This sounds like a family matter," he said. "Do you want me to make a report?"

Mr. Boster shook his head. "No," he said. "Thank you, officer."

The policeman looked sternly down at Haley. "From now on, young lady," he said. "I think it's wise for you to tell your parents where you're going. You had them scared half to death."

"Yes, sir," Haley said, lowering her eyes.

The officer climbed into his car and drove away. Haley looked at her mother and father. "I'm sorry," she said, hanging her head.

"Lauren, Haley, you girls both have some explaining to do," said Mr. Boster, grimly. "Gary, Lauren will be spending the rest of the day at home."

"Yes, sir," Gary said. He walked to his car and drove away. Haley watched him leave, thinking, *Oh no! I'm really going to get in trouble now. I'll be grounded for the rest of my life.*

Haley and Lauren followed their parents into the house. They sat down silently at the kitchen table. Then Mr. Boster cleared his throat.

"Girls," he said. "Tell me what happened."

Haley felt a lump rise to her throat. "I thought Lauren hated me," she explained. "I went to the water tower to catch her."

"It's my fault," Lauren insisted. "I never should have written that in my diary. But I just wanted to see if Haley was still snooping. I never thought anything like this would happen. I forgot that she left for camp today." She sighed and brushed her long hair from her shoulders.

Bit by bit, the story came out as Haley and Lauren each told their side. Mr. and Mrs. Boster listened.

Mrs. Boster shook her head. "I thought you girls had more sense than that," she said. "Lauren, you shouldn't have tricked your sister. And, Haley, I thought you were through with snooping. You've been warned already about it. And you shouldn't have left the house without telling me where you were going."

The telephone rang. Haley was relieved to have the attention taken off of her, even if it was only for a minute. Mrs. Boster answered it. Listening into the receiver, she said, "Yes, she's home. Uh-huh. She's safe. Yes, well I'm sorry, too. Thank you. Good-bye."

Mrs. Boster hung up the phone and turned to Haley. "That was Anna's mother," she said. "They were worried when you weren't at the bus. Anna didn't want to leave without you. The bus waited for you for a few minutes, but then it had to leave to get the other children to camp. They're probably there by now."

Haley thought to herself about camp. She thought about rowing a boat across the lake and sleeping in a cabin. Someone else would get to bunk with Anna now. Other people would hike along the trails. The anticipation of going off to camp had quickly faded away.

Gee, Haley thought to herself. *It's all because I snooped in Lauren's diary. If I hadn't done that, I'd be at camp right now with Anna.*

"I'm done with snooping," Haley decided, shaking her head.

"We're all glad to hear that," said Mrs. Boster with a grin.

"Lauren," said Mrs. Boster. "I hope you'll think twice before you play a trick on your sister again."

"I will, Mom. I'm sorry," Lauren admitted.

The telephone rang, and Mr. Boster answered it. "Lauren, it's for you," he said, and Lauren walked to the telephone.

Haley listened as her sister said, "Hi, Gary. Yeah, everything's okay, now. Tonight? Sure, I'd love to! 8:00?"

Lauren glanced over her shoulder at Haley. Haley leaned her elbows onto the kitchen table. Lauren pressed the receiver against her ear. "Uh, wait a second, Gary," she said. "I think I'll stay home tonight. Yeah, I'd like to spend some time with Haley. I'll see you tomorrow. Okay? All right. Bye."

Haley couldn't believe her ears. Lauren was staying at home—*to be with her.* Haley grinned with happiness.

Lauren left the kitchen. "I'm going to take a shower," she called over her shoulder. "Then, Haley, you and I are going out for ice cream. How does that sound?"

"Great!" exclaimed Haley.

Haley watched as Lauren left the kitchen. Then she turned to her parents, saying, "I'm sorry, Mom and Dad. I didn't mean to cause so much trouble."

"That's okay," Mr. Boster said. "As long as you've learned your lesson about respecting your sister's privacy."

Haley nodded sincerely. "I have, Dad," she said.

Haley walked into the backyard. She crossed the lawn and crawled into the Boy Busters Headquarters. Stretching out on her sleeping bag, she looked over at the empty sleeping bag beside her. Thinking of Anna having fun at camp made her feel a little sad. After all, their club headquarters just wasn't the same without her. *The task of busting boys was too big for one person,* Haley thought to herself.

A drop of sweat trickled down Haley's face. *I'll bet Anna's swimming in the lake,* Haley thought to herself. *Or, maybe she's stepping up to bat on the softball diamond. She and her cabinmates are probably laughing and having a great time by now.*

Haley imagined all the wonderful things she might be missing. And then a happier thought inched its way into her mind. She knew now that Lauren did love her. With a shock, Haley realized that she had finally reached the Boy Buster's goal. After all these weeks of plotting and scheming, the mission was finally accomplished.

"Gary and Lauren are apart," Haley whispered to herself. "Even if it's only for one night. That's what I wanted all along. It'll be just like old times. Me and Lauren, *without Gary.*"

Haley felt a huge relief that something good had resulted from this whole mess. Maybe it was even worth the punishment. After all, being with Lauren was more important than going to camp.

Haley crawled quickly out of the tent. She ran across the lawn and into the house. Racing upstairs, she stopped outside of Lauren's room. She lifted her hand to knock on the door. But Haley stopped her hand in mid air when she heard Lauren's voice. Pressing her ear against the door, Haley could hear the words more clearly.

Lauren was talking on the telephone. "I miss you, too," she said.

"Uh-huh. I'll be thinking about you, too. Bye."

Haley frowned. *It's Gary,* she thought to herself, *again. It looks like Lauren still has Mush Disease.*

Ten

LAUREN seemed distracted the whole night. *This isn't what I wanted*, Haley griped to herself. *Lauren's here, but all she's thinking about is Gary.* It was as if Gary's ghost was haunting their time together. They went to Sally's Soda Shoppe for ice cream. Even there, Lauren pointed out that butter pecan was Gary's favorite ice cream flavor.

Even if the *real* Gary wasn't there, *thoughts* of him certainly were. Lauren spent a lot of time sighing. And Haley was pretty sure that when her sister sighed, Gary was on her mind.

When they got home, Lauren quickly called Gary. Haley wondered if her sister's ear might become permanently flattened from holding it against the telephone receiver. But between these disgusting times, Haley did spend some fun moments with Lauren. During the next week, it almost seemed like old times, with the two of them sitting around in their night-gowns sharing intimate thoughts. Lauren talked about Gary, while Haley talked about softball.

One night they sat together in the quiet of Lauren's bedroom. A cool breeze fluttered through the curtains at the window. Haley sat on the bed with her knees pulled up to her chest. She showed a postcard to Lauren. It was a picture of green pine trees surrounding a sparkling, blue lake. Across the top of the postcard was printed, Hawthorne Ridge Camp.

"Look what I got from Anna," Haley explained. She read the message on the back to Lauren.

Dear Haley,

Camp is great! I wish you were here. Today we had swimming races in the lake. Our team didn't win, but one of the counselors was on my team. His name is Steve. He's really cute, Haley. You wouldn't believe how nice he is for a boy . I took his picture to show you when I get home. See you soon.

Anna

Haley frowned as she read the postcard for the third time. It sounded as if Anna might be catching Mush Disease. Haley decided to have an extra-long Boy Busters meeting when Anna got home. Surely, that would help to get Anna back to normal.

Lauren's blue eyes flashed. "Did I tell you that Gary broke high school records when he was on the swim team?" she asked.

"No," said Haley.

"And," Lauren added, "he plays soccer. He's going to play on the soccer team in college. He got accepted at Missouri State. He even got a partial scholarship."

Is there anything Gary doesn't do? Haley asked herself.

Haley looked at Anna's postcard again. And then she turned her attention back to Lauren. "What are we going to do tomorrow?" asked Haley. "Do you want to go to a movie?"

Lauren smiled. "It's Saturday tomorrow," she said. "Gary and I have a date." Lauren flopped back against her pillow. Her eyes took on a dreamy expression.

"What are you and Gary going to do tomorrow?" asked Haley.

Lauren looked excited. "We're going on a picnic," she said. "Gary's taking me to the state park. He's bringing his guitar, and I'm bringing the sandwiches."

"Oh." Haley's voice was filled with disappointment. She wished that Anna was back from camp. Tomorrow promised to be a lonely day.

Lauren looked closely at Haley. Then suddenly she exclaimed, "Why don't you come with us, Haley?"

"Me?" Haley sat up straighter. "Come along on a date?"

"Sure," said Lauren. "It'll be fun. I'll make extra sandwiches."

Haley hesitated. After all, Boy Busters swore not to go on dates. *But,* Haley told herself, *maybe it didn't matter if it was someone else's date.*

"Okay," said Haley, with a nod. "I'd like to come." She felt excitement tingling her skin inside her. A picnic at the lake sounded like a lot of fun—even if there was going to be a boy along.

* * * * *

When morning came, Haley helped Lauren prepare the picnic food. Haley sliced the tomatoes for the ham sandwiches. There were sandwiches, potato chips, cookies, cheese, and crackers.

"Gary's bringing the lemonade," Lauren said.

Mrs. Boster walked into the kitchen. "You've got enough food for 10 people," she observed. Then with a smile, she added, "I'm glad to see you girls going out together. I hope you have a good time."

The doorbell rang, and Lauren ran to answer it. Haley walked into the living room just in time to see Lauren squeeze Gary's hand. Haley covered her eyes with her fingers. *I hope I don't see a lot of mush this afternoon. I might get sick,* she thought.

Gary carried the bag of picnic supplies out to the car. Mrs. Boster said to Lauren, "Now, you keep an eye on Haley. Don't let her go into the lake. And don't let her wander away. And watch out for snakes and for broken glass."

"Mom," moaned Haley. "Come on. I'm not a baby anymore."

"I guess you're not," said Mrs. Boster.

"You girls grew up so fast. One minute you're babies, and the next minute you have boyfriends."

Haley gave her mother a comforting look. "Don't worry about me, Mom," she said. "I'll *never* like boys!"

Mrs. Boster and Lauren looked at each other over the top of Haley's head. They smiled. Haley thought to herself that they seemed to be sharing a silent secret or joke. *Well, I'll show them,* Haley vowed to herself. *I'm never going to change. I'll always be just the way I am right now.*

Haley followed Lauren out of the house. As Lauren climbed into the front seat of Gary's car, Haley climbed into the back. Gary and Lauren held hands, and Haley held onto the bag of food. Staring straight ahead, Haley remarked again to herself how big Gary's ears were.

Wind rushed around in the car as they

drove away from the house. Soon they had left the town limits and were rolling along country roads. They passed farm houses, fields, and cows. The radio blared, and Haley hummed along with the music.

She watched as Lauren and Gary chatted and laughed together. It was nice to see Lauren smiling. Lauren's cheeks were flushed with pink. Her blue eyes sparkled.

She is happy, Haley thought with a sudden shock. *And I guess some of it is because of Gary.*

Strange thoughts and feelings came into Haley's heart. While she still hated to share Lauren, she did want her to be happy—even if it was with Gary.

He slid his arm along the backseat of the car. His hand closed over Lauren's shoulder. Haley made a monkey face as Lauren smiled at Gary.

Uh-oh, Haley thought, *the mush stuff is still gross.*

Gary pulled the car into the state park and came to a stop near a cluster of trees. He took the food from the car, and Lauren carried a blanket over her arm. Haley lifted the thermos of lemonade from the backseat.

Haley watched as Gary opened the trunk of his car. He pulled out a bat, a glove, and a softball. He handed the softball to Haley.

Haley's eyes widened with surprise. "What's this?" she asked.

Lauren looked down at her little sister. "Oh, didn't I tell you?" she asked. "Gary played a little baseball in high school. He thought you might enjoy playing."

Gary smiled down at Haley. "Lauren says you want to learn to pitch. Do you know how to throw a curve?" he asked.

"No," Haley admitted, shaking her head. She looked carefully at the softball and tossed it back and forth from one hand to the other.

Gary carried the bat and glove in his free hand. "I'll teach you how to pitch if you want me to," he offered, smiling down at Haley.

Haley was stunned. Was this the same boy she had schemed against all these weeks? *Wow, I'm really going to learn to pitch,* she thought.

Haley followed Gary and Lauren through a path in the woods. Soon they came out onto the edge of a big lake. They spread out the blanket by the shore.

While Lauren arranged the food, Gary showed Haley how to hold the softball. "Stretch your finger along the seam," he said. "Hold it like this."

Haley watched him, and then he handed the ball to her. "Here, you try it," he said. "Good. Now you're getting it."

Haley pitched the ball, and Gary caught it. Over and over again they practiced. "I think you're really getting the hang of it, Haley," said Gary. "You're a natural."

Haley beamed from the compliment.

"Whew!" said Gary. "It's really hot. Let's

take a little break, okay?"

Gary settled back onto the blanket next to Lauren. Haley walked to the lake's edge. The sun beamed down. A cool breeze came whisking across the water. Haley smiled to herself.

I guess I don't have to lose my sister, after all, she said to herself. *Gary's great at softball, and he's even helping me. For a boy, he seems okay. But I'm still glad that I'm not old enough to have Mush Disease.*

Haley returned to the blanket and reached for a sandwich. She took a large bite. After she swallowed, she asked, "Do you think I'll be good enough by September that I can try out for the school softball team?"

"Sure," said Gary. "I don't know why not." He reached for the lemonade thermos. "You and I can keep practicing if you want to."

"Okay," said Haley, feeling suddenly shy. She looked from Gary to her sister. Lauren's face was lighted with a big smile.

"That's great!" said Lauren. She squeezed

Haley's hand. She leaned closer and whispered. "See? I told you he'd be your friend if you just let him."

Haley nodded.

Lauren said, "Haley, if you and Gary keep practicing, I'll bet you'll be the best softball player in your class next year."

Haley felt proud. At last, she was on her way to becoming a real pitcher. It wasn't just a dream, anymore.

"Wait until Anna hears about this," she said eagerly. *And just wait until Scott Bailey sees me pitch*, she thought. *He thinks he's so smart.*

Haley stretched back on the blanket. She stuffed a cookie into her mouth and munched. An ant crawled onto her foot, and she wiggled her toes. She smiled at Lauren, and then she stared up at the blue sky deep in thought. She was happy that her sister loved her, and she was really glad that *mushland* was still a long way off.

About the Author

"I remember what it was like to be a kid," says JANET ADELE BLOSS. "I understand how kids feel things very deeply. And I know that kids love to laugh."

Anyone who reads Janet's book will agree that she has a keen insight into the emotional lives of children. The characters in her books live in a kids' world of pesty sisters, creepy brothers, runaway pets, school bullies, and good friends.

The characters laugh, cry, dream, and race through the pages of her stories. As one reader says: "When I read your books, it's like I'm watching a movie."

Janet showed signs of becoming an author as early as third grade when she wrote a story entitled Monkeys on the Moon. By the time Janet reached fifth grade she had decided to become an author. She also wanted to be a flamenco dancer, a spy, a skater for roller derby, and a beach bum in California. But fortunately for her readers it was the dream of becoming an author that came true.

"I've always loved books and children," says Janet. "So writing for children is the perfect job for me. It's fun."

Although Janet's first love is writing, her other interests include dancing, music, camping, swimming, ice-skating, and cats.